FAST & FURIOUS
SPY RACERS
TESTED

by Landry Q. Walker
illustrated by
Patrick Spaziante

CHAPTER 1

Cisco almost dropped his Froyo as he looked up at the enormous and intimidating machine. "You guys are climbing into that thing? For real?"

"Cisco has a point," Frostee added. "This machine is pretty teched-out and all, but the force from being spun that fast in a circle?"

"Right?" Cisco agreed. "You'll be so dizzy, you'll be turned inside out!"

Tony appraised the giant machine and the pod that was attached to it. He couldn't help agreeing with his friends—it didn't exactly look like it would be fun. The rocket-shaped pod was bolted to an arm that was attached to an enormous centrifuge—a machine designed to spin and spin.

A machine that he was supposed to sit inside.

Basically, it was a machine designed to

make you want to hurl your guts out.

"Come on!" Echo Pearl teased. "We've driven off of cliffs. This is totally safe! We'll be fine!" She glanced at the machine. "But you go first."

Ms. Nowhere was looming behind the pair, though she was mostly typing away in some private conversation. Still, she managed to respond with her usual charm. "It's a two-seater," she said. "And you're both getting in it. Together."

Echo's wide smile faded. "Then I find this situation entirely less amusing," the young artist answered.

Tony continued to glance suspiciously at the exceedingly dangerous-looking pod. "We've totally proven ourselves over and over again, right? We've never really failed a mission . . ."

Ms. Nowhere scoffed. "What about that one in San Diego? During Comic-Con? All you had to do was monitor the sale of that experimental fuel filter. Instead . . ."

Tony managed to look hurt. "Totally not

our fault!" he argued. "There were other factors!"

Echo nodded. "There was no way we could know that the submarine was controlled by robots."

"Or that the warehouse was going to be filled with rare movie props," Tony agreed.

"Why would you even put the smuggler ship from *Outspaced 4* in a warehouse?" Frostee added, a rising tone of incredulity in his voice. "It belongs in a museum!"

Cisco raised an eyebrow. "I don't know, man. *Outspaced 4* was not the best in the franchise. Too much of a political agenda."

Layla, who had been otherwise quiet, suddenly looked at her friend. "Oh, don't you start with me, Cisco!" She glared at him. "That movie redefined pop culture!"

"Enough!" Ms. Nowhere roared, stepping between the two teenagers. "It's not up to you to judge the merits of the test. It's up to you to take it!"

"*They* don't have to take it," Tony objected, pointing at Frostee, Cisco, and Layla.

Nowhere rolled her eyes. "Their skills have been tested in a dozen different ways. You're all under examination all the time. That's the way this stuff works when you're a teenager working under adult supervision, okay?"

Both Echo and Tony shifted uncomfortably.

"Your confidence is so incredibly reassuring," Ms. Nowhere said, clearly exasperated. "Cisco, Frostee, Layla, please exit. You can watch the test from the safety of the observation deck."

Before any of them could object, she raised her hand and waved them away.

"Okay," Layla said, giving Tony's shoulder a quick squeeze and throwing a reassuring look at Echo. "You both are going to do great. I'm sure of it."

Frostee shook his head. "I'm *way* less sure of it. But whatever. Hey, Cisco, let's go get some waffles!"

As the three teenagers exited the testing chambers, a stranger walked into the room— a tall man with a white lab coat and thick-framed glasses. "Meet Dr. David Rowan," Ms. Nowhere said. "David is the head engineer and software designer for this testing facility, and he will be monitoring your results."

"Hello, young people," Dr. Rowan said. "Are you ready to begin? My machine will test your limits in ways you cannot even imagine. It'll be fun."

Tony shrugged. "Well, it's totally safe no matter what, right? I mean, we drive cars in the real world. I think we can handle it. It's basically like a theme park ride."

"Perhaps. The controls are fairly self-explanatory," the engineer said with a thin smile. "For a driver of your caliber, I'm sure it should be simple."

"*Pff!*" Tony replied. "Totally, I'm sure."

With that, Ms. Nowhere and Dr. Rowan walked out of the room, and Echo and Tony were left to climb into the strange pod. Inside was a steel cage for reinforcement, and two heavy-looking leather seats with padded harnesses in place. The console was made up of a variety of levers, buttons, and switches. More notably, there were two steering wheels.

The pair strapped themselves in. A moment later, the pod automatically closed itself. In the distance, Tony and Echo both could hear a faint humming, the sound of a very large and very powerful engine warming up.

The voice of David Rowan boomed through the pod's speaker system. *"Everything is ready. The test will begin in ten seconds. I suggest you try to relax. It might get . . . uncomfortable."*

Echo tensed. Tony looked over at her and smiled warmly. He put his hands on the steering wheel. "Don't worry," he said. "We got this thing under—"

But before he could finish his sentence, the massive engine engaged, and the pod began to spin. Two point three seconds later, the pod was whizzing around and around the gigantic room at over four hundred miles per hour, and Tony and Echo began to black out.

CHAPTER 2

Tony felt himself beginning to black out. The pod was spinning impossibly fast. He tried to grab his steering wheel, but it yanked out of his grasp. He glanced over. "Echo?" he managed through gritted teeth. "You okay? I think you gotta turn your wheel when I turn mine."

"Blurg," Echo managed to say. *"Guh,"* she added, for clarity's sake.

"Okay," Tony said as the pod whipped around the massive centrifuge. "We're supposed to do what with this now?"

The light on the dashboard in front of Tony conveniently blinked blue.

"Okay," Tony muttered. "Okay, so I press this and . . ."

Tony pressed the button and immediately wished that he hadn't. The entire pod rotated upside down. Then it began to bounce.

"Dr. Rowan, this is not fun!" Tony heard himself shout.

"Just part of the test," Rowan said through the intercom, with a low chuckle. *"All you have to do is try to maintain your concentration. Focus."*

"Please . . . shut it down," Echo mumbled.

"No!" Tony called as a surge of adrenaline shot through him. "We can do this. Echo, you with me?"

Echo managed a slight shake of her head. "Nope," she said quietly. "Too much spinning."

Tony looked at the control panel. Every light was blinking. Everything was spinning. He felt beyond dizzy.

"So we have to pilot . . . drive . . . steer this stupid pod. And it's a two-person control system." Tony eyed the steering wheels. There was no way he could operate both at the same time. That was the trick! *That* was why the test was so difficult. It took two people operating in perfect synchronicity. "So improvise," Tony managed to say to himself.

With a quick twist, Tony yanked at his belt buckle. The leather belt came free under the heavy seat straps easily enough. Reaching over, Tony looped Echo's steering wheel, twisting it in the process. Then he threaded the belt through a gap in his own steering wheel.

With a deft twist of his wrist, he pulled the belt tight and spun his wheel. Echo's wheel spun in sync. Suddenly, the pod started to stabilize.

Echo struggled to speak. "What?" she mumbled. "You got it?"

"Not quite yet!" Tony shouted.

He noticed the buttons on both consoles were flashing in sequence. The sequence was the same on both consoles.

"Echo!" he yelled. "You need to hit the buttons."

"Okay," she said, still struggling. "Pressing red."

"Now blue," Tony yelled.

"And yellow," Echo added.

"What are you doing?" David Rowan yelled

through the intercom. *"You aren't supposed to be able to do that!"*

"Green!" Tony and Echo both yelled, slamming the last button in the sequence at the same time.

A loud horn sounded in the distance, and the pod slowed to a halt. It opened with a hiss, and the security harness straps automatically released.

Dr. Rowan stormed down the stairs, sweat on his forehead.

"Cheaters!" the engineer yelled. "You cheated! There is no way you could have overcome the disabling effects. My machine is better than any driver!"

Ms. Nowhere followed closely behind. "Rowan! This is completely inappropriate!"

"But they had to have cheated!"

"I'm as surprised as you," Nowhere interjected dryly. "But the test is a challenge of endurance and innovation. *How* they pass isn't an issue."

Dr. Rowan frowned. Tony and Echo were both out of the pod now, though neither was feeling particularly steady on their feet.

"But—" Rowan started.

"No," Ms. Nowhere mused. "I found this very illuminating. David, put together a full report of the process they used to shut the machine down."

The engineer threw one last look of anger at Tony, then stormed off.

"So, did we pass?" Tony asked Ms. Nowhere. "I mean, we did it! We took control of the thing and we passed, right?"

Ms. Nowhere tapped her foot. "I'm not unimpressed with your performance, Tony. Head to the debriefing chambers and we will discuss your results."

"Awesome!" Tony said, smiling. "You hear that, Echo? We did great! Come on, let's go chill."

Tony headed for the door, with a wide smile on his face, but Ms. Nowhere reached out and placed a hand on Echo's shoulder, stopping the young girl from following her friend.

"One moment, Echo," Ms. Nowhere started to say.

"You don't need to say it," Echo murmured. "I know . . . I wasn't good enough."

And with that, Echo followed Tony out the door.

CHAPTER 3

"You see that?" a voice whispered. "They both responded so differently. Is that—"

"It's within the predictive norms. The test's reactions are always different, based on the individual. But the metrics of the results remain consistent."

"You're certain? This needs to be a fair assessment or it's meaningless."

"One hundred percent. If the reaction was identical, that would be a much larger concern. The nature of this . . ." The man speaking took a moment and adjusted a dial on a large computer console. In response, a series of lights fluctuated. Satisfied, he continued. "The point is, the story that unfolds for each subject is driven by the subconscious of the individual. Just wait, you'll see."

"And they are completely locked in their hypnotic states?"

"That's what the pod really does. They think they've already completed the test, but they'll keep spinning for as long as we need them to. They will see and feel everything as if they were somewhere else. And we can monitor *that* reaction."

Ms. Nowhere nodded. "Okay, then, Dr. Rowan. Let's continue."

CHAPTER 4

Tony felt on top of the world. He had aced the test, apparently breaking all the records of endurance as he did so. Then he had gorged himself at the ice-cream bar, spent a couple of hours playing video games, and even read the newest issue of his favorite comic book, *Gamma Blast Three*. It was a pretty great day.

And then the power went out.

Which was a weird thing to happen in the lair of a government shadow operation.

Tony poked his head out of the rec room. It was quiet. Where had everyone gone? He tapped his spy watch. "Hey, Layla? Echo?" Nothing. Just static. "Ms. Nowhere?" he tried. Still nothing.

And then the static broke, and a deep voice hissed at him through his spy watch. *"No one is here to help you, Tony. No way for you to cheat, either."*

Tony blinked. "Rowan? Dr. Rowan, right?" The lights flickered. The hallway of the facility was empty. "Hey, Dr. Rowan. What's going on?"

At the end of the hallway, a monitor switched on, and it broadcast the very angry face of Dr. Rowan.

"That test was my life's work. It was everything to me. I built a machine that was unbeatable."

"I mean, you really didn't," Tony replied.

"You cheated! The test was supposed to be defeated by two people, working in tandem, as a team. You bypassed that with your little belt trick!"

The monitor started moving. Tony squinted. It was attached to . . .

"A robot?" Tony said, taking a step backward. "Is that a robot?"

"No, Tony Toretto," Rowan said, his voice filled with menace. *"It's your doom."*

CHAPTER 5

Echo slammed on the pedal of her car as she sped toward the beach. The sleek electric hot rod hugged the road tightly, speeding around each corner with a smooth pull, even at a high speed. The g-force of the turns was nothing. She did this stuff every day! Why had it been so hard on the crazy, topsy-turvy pod? And why had it been so much easier for Tony?

Echo's thoughts were derailed as another car—a heavy-looking muscle car polished to an almost mirrorlike state of perfection—roared past her. It was a modern classic style, a wide-framed beast of a car with a custom plate that read T0B1A5. Exactly the kind of distraction Echo needed.

Echo smiled to herself. This was going to be too easy. She angled her foot slightly, and with an electric whine, her car surged up next to the powerful-looking muscle car.

The muscle car eased down, stopping at a red light, and a lanky young man with a mop of curly golden hair leaned over his passenger seat to hit Echo with a lopsided grin.

"Sweet ride!" the smiling youth yelled over the roar of his engine. "Up for a challenge?"

Echo almost laughed. Her car was a hyperfueled custom job engineered by the best mechanics working for Ms. Nowhere. Then she looked at the muscle car again. It had a semitransparent hood, with an array of spinning lights whirling underneath. The wheels had spinners, with another spinner built inside. Everything about the hot rod screamed custom job. Maybe it wouldn't be such an easy race after all. Or maybe that was her lack of confidence, whispering in her ear.

"I guess you're Tobias?" Echo said, based on his license plate.

"You got that right. And I've got more heat on this block than you've got in that toy you're wheeling in."

Echo let the electric engine of her car roar.

"Okay, then, Tobias, let's see what you got!"

The light turned green, and both cars screeched down the road, leaving streaks of black rubber behind them. The two cars sped down the unusually empty beachside highway.

The boy was a skilled driver; that much was obvious. And his car was impressive. But this shouldn't have even been a contest. Echo had proven herself as a driver over and over—and not in some stupid pod test. She had raced *real* cars against *real* racers. Driving was an art form, and Echo was the artist.

A hairpin turn was approaching, and Echo's car hugged the road as always, but she felt her foot easing up on the pedal. Her skin flushed with anxiety. "Weird," she muttered to herself.

She still felt dizzy. The next thing she knew, everything went black. And her car began to spin . . . and spin . . . and spin . . .

CHAPTER 6

Tony narrowly dodged a laser beam from David Rowan's killer robot. It was a clunky silver machine, with two arms and two legs, and a gigantic monitor strapped to its chest. On the monitor was the face of Dr. Rowan.

"You fool!" Rowan cackled cartoonishly. *"You may have cheated your way through the pod, but I have a hundred other inventions to destroy you with! Like these missiles!"*

The robot fired a small barrage of missiles from its shoulders, which tore past Tony and blew a hole in the wall. Rather than wait to see what the robot unleashed next, Tony opted to jump through the hole and get out of the path of destruction. Tony mentally checked where he could be. The hallway that he had been in led to a series of meeting rooms and staff facilities. The hole in the wall should lead directly to a briefing . . .

"Nope," Tony said. "This is totally not right."

It was, in fact, very wrong. The ceiling of the briefing room had apparently been removed and replaced with a series of shifting platforms, each moving in and out of the wall. It was like—

"It's like a video game," Tony whispered.

Another monitor flickered on. David Rowan's angry face appeared. *That's right! It is a game. A game you can't cheat at. A game you* can't *win. And when you fail, I'll prove that I am the best engineer to ever grace these halls!*

"These halls?" Tony yelled. "How did you change the entire building? And where is everyone?"

"I created a distraction, emptying the building so that only we remained," Rowan bragged. *"And I built this entire complex. I designed every wall, every door, every window. And within it, I secretly created the perfect test. The* impossible *test! The test that will lead to your defeat!"*

CHAPTER 7

Echo blinked as she regained consciousness. For a moment, she had forgotten where she was, and had almost expected to wake up and find herself back in that stupid pod.

But instead, Tobias was looming over her. "You okay?" he asked. "You started to spin out."

Echo sat up abruptly, pushing him aside. "My car! Where's my—" It was sitting five feet away, completely intact. Echo's brow furrowed. "How . . . I was spinning out—"

Tobias stood, reaching out a hand to help Echo up. "You pulled out of the spiral just in time. I don't know how you did it, but I've never seen anyone drive like that."

Echo shook off her disorientation. "Seriously? I couldn't have managed that during the test?"

Tobias blinked. "Sorry, what?"

"Nothing," Echo replied, feeling mildly embarrassed. "Thanks, I guess . . . You pulled me out of the car?"

"You looked like you needed some air," he answered. "You okay now?"

"Yeah, I think so. My name's Echo, by the way," she said, reaching out her hand.

"Tobias Grube," he answered as he shook her hand. "You new in town?"

"Not really." Echo looked around. "Where exactly am I? Where is the city?"

Tobias laughed. "You're basically between nowhere and nothing. It's a good stretch to race on, though. Maybe you want a rematch?"

Echo shrugged. "Maybe." But then a slash of lightning in the air distracted her.

In the distance, illuminated for only a second, was an old mansion on a hill.

"What is that place?" she asked.

"Just a dusty old art gallery. Nothing great," Tobias said dismissively.

"An art gallery in the middle of nowhere in

a spooky mansion?" Echo said, with one thin eyebrow raised. "And I'm *not* supposed to go look? I don't think so."

CHAPTER 8

Tony tried to grab one of the old-school emergency phones. Unfortunately, as soon as he grabbed a receiver, David Rowan's robot fired out a pencil-thin laser that severed the physical line.

"Tsk, tsk," Rowan's voice sang through the speakers. *"This game won't be so easily cheated!"*

Tony stepped back, taking in the room. The platforms shifted at a furious speed, but they did so in a rhythm.

"Hesitating, Tony?" Rowan mocked. *"I can see why. A simple race car driver like you could never possibly manage to defeat my doomsday traps!"*

That was the last bit of motivation Tony needed to jump into action, running toward the wall at a breakneck pace. At the last moment before collision, he leaped up and kicked his feet against the opposing wall to his right. He bounced across the narrow hallway, back and forth, letting his momentum propel him upward, high enough to grab the edge of the bottom platform.

That's when Tony heard a whooshing sound and saw a panel in the wall open—and from that panel, boiling water began pouring out, quickly filling the hallway below!

"You can run, Tony Toretto," Rowan said, his voice menacing and low. *"But you can't hide."*

CHAPTER 9

"This is some amazing art," Echo said as she wandered through the gallery with Tobias. "Check this one out. It's called *Saira*. It's beautiful! I can't believe I've never heard of this gallery. You'd think—" Echo's train of thought was interrupted by the sound of an alarm.

And then suddenly the lights went out.

Echo whirled in the direction of a sound. Something swift swooshed past her with a rush of air. She couldn't see, but the sound was unmistakable—a drone!

Echo slapped on the emergency light built into her spy watch and shined it in a fast three-hundred-and-sixty-degree sweep.

"Tobias?" she called out, but the stranger was gone. The drone, however, was as clear as day: a gleaming black piece of hardware that would have made Frostee jealous. The machine had four arms built into it, remote robotics of some kind. More important, it had the *Saira* painting in its polished claws.

"No way," Echo muttered to herself. "A high-tech art robbery?"

She sprang into action, but the drone sailed through the air faster than she could run. Just as she started to sprint, a dozen armed guards surrounded her, stepping between Echo and the escaping drone. A split second later, the remote-control robot rocketed right out a window to freedom, with the painting in tow.

"Hands up!" the guards yelled as they pointed their stun weapons at her. Echo had no choice. In the distance, she could see the robot flying away through the night sky. And then she noticed something weirder . . . The stolen painting was still hanging on the wall!

CHAPTER 10

Tony realized the ceiling was much higher than he'd thought. The moving platforms were the only way up. Down was no longer an option, with the rising level of boiling water filling in.

He glanced down and almost stumbled but steadied himself and jumped once more, grabbing the platform above with an outstretched hand.

"You seriously think that creating a real-life video game is gonna stop me?" the teenager said, laughing. "I rule at games! I play them, like, way too much! Layla even called my skills 'dangerous for my development'! That's how awesome I am."

The voice of David Rowan roared from a nearby speaker built into the wall. *"That's not a good thing!"*

Then circular saw blades spun out of the wall!

"Too slow!" Tony laughed as he dodged them. But one blade came a little too close, and Tony began to slip.

"Getting tired?" Rowan taunted. *"My machines never will!"*

Tony grabbed one of the blades that had lodged in the wall and ripped it free. With a quick spin of his wrist, he flung the serrated metal disk toward a sealed door.

The heavy blade tore through the door and created an exit from the never-ending climb that Tony was struggling with.

Tony dove through the hole, narrowly avoiding another missile attack. He was in a new room now, though it looked pretty much identical to the old one. Tony couldn't help wondering just how big this building was.

And then, with a slight whooshing sound, *another* panel opened and a bunch of snakes fell out. A whole bunch. Like hundreds and hundreds of hissing, writhing, sinister-looking snakes.

"Aaaah!" yelled Tony.

CHAPTER 11

It had taken only a quick call to Ms. Nowhere to clear things up with the security team, though it seemed to Echo as if it had been an eternity. But at least during that eternity, Echo had gotten a sense of who was who and what exactly was going on.

"This is the third painting stolen in the last three weeks!" cried the dark-haired Susan Damon, the curator of the museum. "And every time it's the same! The drone cuts the power, flies in, and flies back out with the art!"

"And they always leave a fake painting in place of the original, too. Plastic replicas!" lamented Ricky Lovas, an elderly man with white hair and a goatee.

"Why leave a fake at all?" Echo replied.

Susan shook her head. "It slows us down usually, trying to find which wing of the museum was robbed. The security grid shows us everything is in place."

"Except this time, there was a witness," Ricky said. "And she saw the drone *and* the criminal. Maybe we can actually catch this guy now!"

"I can trace the drone with my spy watch," Echo suggested. "They're pinging an IP address, and the signal seems to be coming from the south, down the coast."

Ricky frowned. "But the boy—"

Echo shrugged. "If I find the drone, it might lead to Tobias and the paintings. I'll be back soon."

CHAPTER 12

"Interesting," Ms. Nowhere said as she watched the semiconscious, hypnotized forms of Echo and Tony through a monitor. The pair were still whizzing around in circles in the pod, completely unaware that everything they were experiencing was part of a false reality generated by the spinning and the flashing lights.

"The story that each subject is experiencing is created out of their own subconscious," Dr. Rowan explained. "Mr. Toretto doesn't seem to like me very much," he added.

"You were introduced as an authority figure." Nowhere nodded. "His rebellious streak is strong. Echo, on the other hand—"

"Her imagination has created quite an elaborate scenario," Rowan noted as he analyzed the data.

"She's daydreaming about art thieves and mystery stories. Completely on point for her." Nowhere sighed. "Hopefully, both of them can work through their personal demons." She twisted a dial, and the centrifuge spun faster. "I'd hate to see either of them fail," she said.

CHAPTER 13

"You're going to fail!" yelled a twenty-foot-long snake with Rowan's face on it. It wasn't a real snake, of course, but some kind of crazy robot snake that the mad scientist had cooked up. There were also dozens of smaller robot snakes, all trying to bite Tony at every turn.

Tony ran down the long hallway, rounding the corner as fast as he could. Behind him the giant snake slithered along the carpet, propelling its metal form forward.

Without missing a step, Tony pulled his spy watch off, tapping furiously at the buttons on the device.

"You trying to make a call, cheater? Hoping your friends can bail you out? The entire building is cell-signal shielded. You'll have to figure this one out for yourself."

Tony whirled. The robot was almost on him. "Okay, Dr. Snake-bot. Well, how about this, then?" With a quick flip of the wrist, he threw the watch at the snake. It hit the metal forehead of the monster.

Rowan's voice came through speakers built into the robot. *"What exactly did you hope to—"*

Suddenly the spy watch overloaded, sending out a pulse signal. It had been a long shot, but Tony remembered a briefing lesson when they had been taught not to reset the spy watch while they were sitting on a metal surface.

The robot snake emitted a bunch of smoke. All the tiny snakes suddenly died, too.

Tony picked up his watch. It was rebooting, but still functional, luckily. With a quick look, he checked out the hallway he was in. It didn't have the infinitely high ceiling the other did. So . . . where exactly was he supposed to go now?

Then a hatch in the ceiling opened up and a spiral staircase dropped down.

"You built stairs in your super-doomsday tower?" Tony laughed as he launched himself

up the twisting staircase. "You're not even trying anymore!"

Rowan's voice rang out. *"You think it will be so easy?"* he roared.

Suddenly the stairs flattened into smooth slopes. Tony started to slide back down. Now he was in immediate danger of plummeting all the way to the bottom, where a pit of razor-sharp spikes awaited.

CHAPTER 14

Echo traced the drone signal down the coast, all the way to a rickety, waterlogged pier.

She couldn't help shuddering. The location was remote, and the waters off the docks were completely still. The moon was low and gave off little light, but Echo could see a small device duct-taped to one of the rotting timbers.

It was a signal repeater. The signal Echo was following—this was a false trail and probably a trap! Suddenly, Echo's thoughts were interrupted by a very familiar hum.

"Tobias?" she asked as she turned. Though she already suspected what she would see.

Sure enough, three drones swarmed her. They were just like the one she had seen in the art gallery, but instead of hands at the end of their arm attachments, they had—

"Blasters?" Echo said, surprised.

The drones opened fire. It *was* a trap! Echo

jumped to the left, barely avoiding the deadly assault. The wooden structure of the pier swayed under her feet. One of the stabilizing beams must have been shattered by the blasts.

Seeing an opportunity, Echo dove through a freshly created hole in the pier, knowing that the drones would try to follow. Instantly, three of them zoomed through the hole after her. But Echo hadn't allowed herself to hit the water. Instead, she had caught the beam with one hand and twisted her body so that she was nestled safely on a damp beam running horizontally under the pier. It was a gamble. She wasn't really hidden. There wasn't really anywhere to hide. But she wasn't where the drones would expect her to be. All she could do was hope that the machines' momentum would take care of the problem for her.

Mostly, it worked. Two of the drones crashed into the calm ocean, but the third had course corrected. That's when Echo leaped out from the pier understructure and onto the top of the last drone. The hovering machine scanned the water below and, not finding

Echo, concluded that its job was done. Its sensors couldn't register the girl riding on top of it, so it prepared to return itself to its base.

Soon, Echo would find the lair of whoever was stealing the paintings. Tobias, or someone else . . .

CHAPTER 15

Tony tumbled down the spiral staircase toward the spikes. He was dizzy almost immediately. But this wasn't the first time Tony had almost fallen to his doom, and he quickly slapped at his spy watch, unleashing the grappling hook built within.

The grapple fired from the end of the muzzle, and the hook launched up into the distance. The rope went taut. It had latched on to something! Tony pushed a button on the tiny handle, and the thin rope began to retract, pulling him up, out of immediate danger, but toward Dr. Rowan.

Between him and Dr. Rowan, though, was a glass ceiling.

As Tony twisted his wrist in just the right way, his spy watch responded by reeling in the grappling hook and speeding Tony up toward the thin glass ceiling.

Too fast, Tony thought. *Gotta think fast!*

He quickly reached into his pocket and grabbed the first thing he found—a spare spark plug with a hard ceramic and metal housing. Just what he needed! A moment before his body would crash through the glass, he flung the spark plug above him, shattering the ceiling a split second before it would have sliced him to ribbons. Then he sailed through the gap and rolled to his feet.

Rowan was there with a series of computers stretched out in front of him. In his hand was a remote control.

"You . . . you can't," Rowan started to say.

Tony wasted no time and knocked the remote out of the villain's grasp. It plummeted through the hole in the glass floor to the depths of the staircase below.

Tony whirled, ready for the final battle.

CHAPTER 16

Echo rode the drone all the way back to the last place it should have flown to—the art gallery.

More specifically, the warehouse at the back of the gallery. Once she docked into the drone's recharging station, Echo used the light on her spy watch to investigate the dusty, dark building.

There was a lot of odd stuff around—piles of newspapers, a rack of old clothes—but most notably a large printer with a heavy spool of some kind of thin plastic attached to it, and a pile of paintings that looked way too nice to be stored loosely inside a dusty warehouse.

Then Echo heard a familiar voice.

"Tobias?" she called out. Echo looked down and discovered a clear seam in the wooden floor. Pulling on a small hole in the wood, she revealed a hidden staircase.

At the bottom of the makeshift hideaway was the boy she had been seeking. But one look at the teenager, and it was clear Tobias was not the thief.

Echo quickly pulled the gag from Tobias's mouth and untied his wrists. "Are you okay?" she asked.

"I don't know what happened," Tobias said as he rubbed his arms. "Everything went dark and I woke up here, wherever this is."

Before Echo could reply, the drone came back to life. It was clear that it now knew where Echo was, and it was intent on ending her, and Tobias.

"Look out!" Echo yelled, shoving the still-disoriented boy out of the line of fire.

Tapping some buttons on her spy watch, Echo activated a flare that fired across the room. The drone was distracted by the light and spun toward it. Echo didn't hesitate. She jumped at the drone recharging station. It was a long shot, but the charging station was probably the "brain" of the drone. If it wasn't encrypted, her spy watch could override the remote systems!

Echo's watch lit up with the drone controls. Quickly, she sent a command.

The drone floated, then turned to flash a spotlight on a nearby figure—Ricky Lovas!

That's when the art gallery's alarms started blaring, and Echo knew that everything would be over soon.

CHAPTER 17

"You win, okay? Is that what you want? Are you happy now?" Dr. Rowan said, moping.

"Wait. What's happening?" Tony asked, confused. "Are we still fighting?"

"I can't do it!" Rowan said through tears. "I can't beat you! I'm the one who failed."

"Am I supposed to feel bad?" Tony said, even more confused. "You were trying to kill me!"

Rowan shook his head. "It was all just part of *my* test, to see if I could keep working at the agency. I can't even build a security system that can stop a teenager!"

"But the robots and the threats . . ." Tony shook his head.

"Just part of the act. Half of it was holographic projection anyway. None of it could hurt you. When Ms. Nowhere finds out . . ."

"Just hold on. We can work this out," Tony said, patting Rowan on the shoulder in an attempt to comfort the overwrought engineer.

And that's when Rowan grabbed a second remote control—one connected to a long extension cord—and began pressing buttons.

"You foolish child! You thought you defeated me? This robot, my final robot, is truly unstoppable!"

Except that nothing happened.

Rowan looked down at the remote and kept pressing buttons. "I don't understand," he said in a much more subdued voice. "Where's my giant killer robot?"

Tony shrugged, holding up an unplugged extension cord that ran from the remote, which Rowan was holding, to the wall. "I noticed your remote kind of looked like another secret weapon. So when I patted your shoulder, I kicked it from the socket." Tony gave the scientist a lopsided smile. "Sorry, but listen," Tony continued, dropping the cord. "Look at everything you built here! You're an amazing engineer! So I managed not to pass out in the spinning pod. You built it so it could be beaten. Just like you built everything in this building so I could escape it."

"W-well," Rowan stammered. "I mean . . ."

"Like the platforms? Why build those at all if all you wanted to do was win? No, they were there so I could be challenged," Tony said, realizing it now. "You built a great death-trap building! You don't need to defeat me; you're already so winning! Seriously!"

Rowan blushed awkwardly. "Hey, thanks. I kinda did try to destroy you, though."

Tony grabbed the scientist by the shoulders. "Let's let them think you beat me! Only a little, though. So you, like, barely beat me?"

"You would cheat," Rowan asked, his jaw dropping, "to save my job?"

"I guess so. I know you don't like cheating . . . but you *are* a good engineer. You really had me going in there! And together, I bet we could create the coolest video game ever, you know?"

"If you're sure . . . ," Dr. Rowan said, hesitating.

But Rowan's voice was sounding farther away now.

And another, more distant voice of Ms. Nowhere could be heard. "Okay, that should do it. Wake them up!"

And then suddenly everything went white.

CHAPTER 18

"What is the meaning of this!" shouted Susan Damon, the museum's curator, as she burst into the warehouse storage room.

Echo gestured at the pile of paintings. "Check it," she said. "I think you'll find your missing art isn't as missing as you thought. And if you search your employee here, I think you'll find a remote for controlling the drones."

Ricky glanced uncomfortably at the pile. "Those are the fakes," he sneered. "We put them here for now. She'll say anything to save her little friend. She's probably in on it all!"

"Then how about we look at your fingernails," Echo said, pointing. "Those fake plastic paintings? I have a feeling we'll find some of the same plastic used on those 'fakes' under your nails. The same plastic that's hooked up to this printer!"

With that, Echo pulled back the tarp on the printer, unveiling it.

Susan was dumbfounded. "That's . . . you mean . . . ?"

Echo nodded. "The drones never took the actual paintings. Instead, they covered them with a thin plastic fake. Then Ricky would take them out here so he could 'dispose' of them. In other words, sneak them out undetected!"

"But why?" Susan asked, completely baffled.

"What did you expect, Susan?" he yelled. "You know I could run this gallery better than you! Why, I could transform it into a destination gallery of modern art unlike any other! But no, everything always has to be your way!" Ricky pulled a dangerous-looking device from his jacket. A light on the controls began blinking. "Let's see how you handle your way out of this!"

Susan started to argue, but Echo was quick to pull her back. "Wait!" Echo cried out. "That's a cascading pulse bomb! If it goes off—"

"Everything goes boom!" Ricky said, sneering. "All of you, the art, the entire building!"

"Just deactivate the bomb, Ricky," Echo said, trying to sound intimidating. "No one has to get hurt."

"Never!" Ricky said, flinging the bomb and running away. The bomb blinked. It was active. It was going to explode.

Echo almost froze. Her arms and legs felt heavy. Her body wanted to shut down. It was like the pod test all over again, except this time, there was no safety measure to shut it down and no teammate to lend a hand. There was only her, no one else. No one was going to save the day. Unless she did.

Echo leaped into action, grabbing the bomb and running with it. The explosion would be huge, but if she could get far enough away, Tobias and Susan and all the art could be safe.

She could feel the bomb warming up in her hand. She knew it would explode any second.

So she jumped out the window. It was the only way. She would plummet down the cliffside toward the ocean. But everyone else would be safe.

And then everything went white, and Echo was certain this was the end.

Until she heard a voice in the distance.

Ms. Nowhere?

"Okay, that should do it. Wake them up!"

EPILOGUE

The pod slowly ground to a halt. The semiconscious forms of Echo and Tony were carefully removed.

In only a few minutes the pair were awake, and both were completely disoriented.

"It wasn't real?" Tony said moments later. "But it felt . . ." He looked up and saw David Rowan standing nearby. He glanced over at Ms. Nowhere and beckoned her closer. "Are we one hundred percent sure? Because I'm almost positive that guy there might be, like, super evil . . ."

Overhearing, Rowan laughed in a friendly voice as he reached out to shake Tony's hand. "I promise you, I'm not a super villain. I designed the hypnotic pod that induced your dream state. And I have to compliment you, Tony. Your imagination is quite fierce. Maybe we should make a video game together!"

71

"Okay?" Tony said as he shook the offered hand.

"So wait," Echo cut in. "That whole thing where I passed out and Tony did everything himself—"

"A bit of shared consciousness via gentle suggestion," Ms. Nowhere said. "Neither of you was awake inside that pod for more than a few seconds. The rest of the scenarios spun out of your own subconscious."

"Yeah," Echo replied, shaking her head. "I get that. But did we pass the test?"

Ms. Nowhere shrugged. "The test? The spinning machine was just to help induce the hypnosis state. The real test was the choices you made."

Tony jumped in. "But Echo got to race in her test! I didn't get to race! So it's not really fair—"

"It's not a win-or-lose scenario," Ms. Nowhere answered. "You were presented with choices, facing your own strengths and weaknesses. The decisions you made were informative."

"We did beat the bad guys, though," Tony said. "So we must have done pretty good?"

Ms. Nowhere waved her hand dismissively. "Again, it was informative. The data will be examined and added to your profile. If it makes you feel better, neither of you let us down."

"All I know is that I need some sleep," Echo lamented.

"I should have known it wasn't real," Tony grumbled.

And then the conversation was interrupted by a loud crash and a shout.

"Ms. Nowhere! This is outrageous!" Layla yelled, storming in with Frostee and Cisco behind her. She was *mad*. Her hair was also green . . . as was most of the rest of her. And she was covered in feathers.

Ms. Nowhere sighed. "Do I even want to know?"

"In our defense," Frostee began, "we didn't know the paint would fall right where she was standing."

"And the feathers shouldn't have been that sticky," Cisco added.

"I am going to hurt them," Layla fumed. "This is understood, right? One day, when they least expect it."

"All of you get cleaned up or go rest or something. We still have a lot of data to examine and work to do," Ms. Nowhere said.

The group of kids made their way out, though Tony, the last to slip through the door, managed one last question.

"But we won, right?" he asked. "We passed the test?"

Ms. Nowhere pressed a button on her watch, and the door automatically closed in the young racer's face. She dusted off her sleeves and turned to David Rowan.

"This," she said, "is why I didn't become a teacher. Imagine this every day."

"I don't think most teachers place their students in hypnotically induced trances," Dr. Rowan countered.

Ms. Nowhere picked up a data pad and began typing. "The truth of it is they both did quite well. Tony managed to overcome some of his impulsive behavior, plus he showed compassion. Echo overcame her own self-doubt."

"They also both had some red flags," Rowan pointed out.

"They both have great potential, though," Nowhere said. "But it really comes down to which one of them is ready today." She paused over their names on her pad. Then she looked up at Dr. Rowan. "I know who it has to be. There's only one choice, really." She gave a sly smile as she checked a box. "But what do you think?" she asked. "Which one did I pick?"